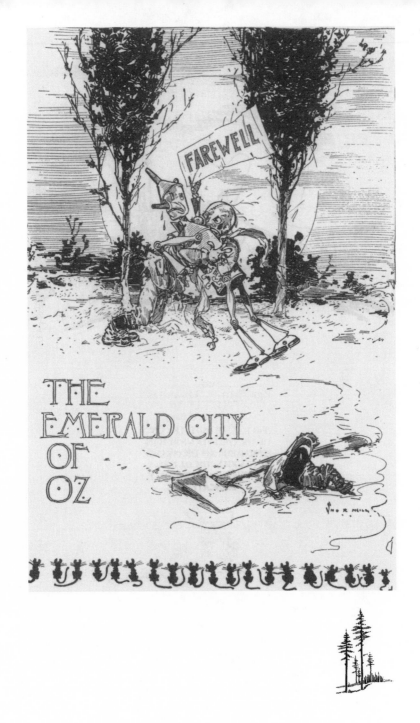

THE
EMERALD CITY
OF
OZ

Ambassador Leroux had to read the message three times to understand what the undersecretary was saying. *It must be a practical joke from one of those idiots in the Department,* he thought, and asked for the telegram to be sent again. Unfortunately for the ambassador, the instructions remained unchanged. To Oscar's delight, the ambassador called at his apartment with a bouquet of flowers and some good news.

"I may have been a little hasty and said a few things in the heat of the moment I didn't really mean when you announced your plans to marry Rosa. Now, after careful reflection and consultations with the Department, I have come to give you my personal blessing and — this is very important, Oscar — to provide my formal approval, in my capacity as Her Majesty's Ambassador Plenipotentiary and Extraordinary to the Republic of Colombia, for your marriage."

Although Oscar in his moments of sobriety was not actually in that much of a rush to get married, and Rosa, not speaking any language known in Bogota, had no idea what was going on, the marriage was held within the month at the seminary of the Saints of the Holy Apostles, a Canadian order of priests in Bogota. The Colombian authorities were at first amused when the Canadian embassy applied by diplomatic note for a marriage licence. They thought the Canadians were not being serious and were making a joke at their expense; an unusual joke perhaps, but a joke nevertheless; these gringos sometimes had a strange sense of humour. But when they sent a note denying the request, the ambassador called on the foreign minister to make representations, and the undersecretary called in the Colombian ambassador in Ottawa and did the same thing.

"Just think of the symbolic value," they told the Colombians. "Such a marriage would symbolize the union between the Indians of Canada and Colombia and provide a new foundation for relations between our two countries."

And so, although Rosa had no birth certificate and no one, including herself, knew her age, the Colombian government directed the Ministry of the Interior to overlook the rules and issue a marriage licence to the betrothed and an exit permit to Rosa. Indians, after all, were just Indians and the Colombians really didn't care what happened to her.

The entire Canadian embassy staff, including a smirking Pilar, attended the wedding. Although invited, most diplomatic representatives stayed away because the dean of the diplomatic corps, a former dictator who had enjoyed imprisoning and torturing his opponents when he was leader of his country, had let his colleagues know he thought such a marriage would undermine the high ethical standards diplomats occupied in the social structure of Latin American society. A dozen or more members of the foreign ministry accepted their invitations, but did not come. The Canadian priest who performed the service was puzzled when Rosa didn't seem to understand when he asked her at the appropriate part of the ceremony if she took Oscar to be her lawful wedded husband. In the end, it all worked out and Oscar and Rosa flew to Ottawa with their wedding presents in time to celebrate Thanksgiving together as the leaves turned colour in the Gatineau Hills, and they began their new lives as man and wife.

4

The two years Oscar would spend in Ottawa before being posted abroad again would not be happy ones. While the senior officers were prepared to overlook his conduct in Colombia, the other ranks were not as forgiving. Their view was that Oscar had used his Indian identity for personal advantage, and not knowing that his odd behaviour had been triggered by the collapse of his relationship with Claire, they thought his passion for human rights had affected his judgement. When Oscar reported for duty, his staffing officer congratulated him coldly on his marriage and exiled him to Information Division in the basement of the East Block to draft letters for the signature of the minister to schoolchildren who wanted information on life overseas for their school projects but who were too lazy to do their own research.

His marriage, Oscar soon discovered, while not an absolute failure, did not live up to his hopes. For one thing, it turned out that Rosa was not pregnant.

"It's just amoebas and parasites she's picked up from drinking the water back where she comes from," the doctor said after conducting a few tests. "That's why her stomach is so swollen. In a few weeks or months, after taking a few pills, she should be back to normal."

And so she was, to the distress of the newly married couple. Since Rosa, despite much effort, made no progress in learning to speak English, they passed their time in their respective solitudes, made worse by Oscar's drinking and Rosa's deepening homesickness. Rosa spent her days looking out the window, and Oscar, to avoid the painful atmosphere at home, began to stay at his desk after hours reading books borrowed from the library and quietly sipping *aguardiente* from the stock he had brought back from Colombia.

Then one morning in the spring of 1956, Luigi sent Oscar a telegram saying a death squad had killed Rosa's parents in a raid on their encampment, and that the members of her extended family had fled into exile across the Orinoco River into Venezuela. Oscar immediately sent a telegram to Luigi saying he intended to return with Rosa to Colombia and search for her family. But that same afternoon, Luigi replied, telling him not to come. The remnants of her family, Luigi wrote, were so well hidden in the jungle that no one would ever find them.

For hours that evening, Oscar tried to tell Rosa that her parents were dead but she gave no sign she understood. He then obtained a copy of a *National Geographic* magazine with colour photos documenting the lives of South American Indians. One of the photos was a burial scene with mourning members of a family gathered around a body. Oscar shook Rosa by the shoulder to obtain her attention, showed her the picture of the downcast men, women, and children around the corpse, pointed to her and pretended he was crying. Rosa looked at him, not understanding. Oscar drew her attention to the photograph again, and pretended to cry again. He then took one of her hands and rubbed her eyes with it, and Rosa began to cry. But her tears did not provoke catharsis and she stopped eating. Afraid she was intent on starving herself to death, Oscar prepared meals of rice, beans, and fried bananas — her favourite foods — but they no longer interested her. Oscar did not know what to do and neither did the doctors.

"She's grieving and misses her family," they said. "Take her back to her people for a visit." But when Oscar said her family was either dead or hiding in the Venezuelan jungle, the doctors said they couldn't do anything for her. It was by then summer, and in desperation Oscar took her to the Indian Camp hoping she would feel more at home among his people. Friends and relatives gathered around, telling Oscar he should have brought Rosa to see them when they first arrived from Colombia. The old people said Rosa looked like Louisa before she passed away, and everyone said she was a younger version of Stella.

"You married your mother and grandmother," someone said, but Oscar did not join in the laughter. "My wife is grieving for her dead family, and if she doesn't start eating, she'll die."

"Take her to see the Manido of the Lake," an old woman said, "and when you come back we'll have a feast prepared."

Although he didn't believe it would do any good, Oscar borrowed a canoe and paddled down the river and out onto Lake

Muskoka. Pulling up beside the blind statue, he threw some tobacco on the water, raised his hands in the air, and uttered a prayer.

"Oh Great Manido of the Lake," he intoned. "I have been away for many years and have returned home with a Native woman from another land who is sad because her family is dead. Use your powers to make her well, Oh Great Manido, and I'll come more often to see you."

Rosa, who had watched Oscar throw the tobacco on the water and say his prayer, smiled for the first time since she arrived in Canada, and on their return to the Indian Camp, she broke her fast and ate the fried fish, bannock, and wild blueberries the women had prepared for her. But when it came time to return to Ottawa, Rosa went into the shack, took a chair at the table in front of the window looking out over Port Carling Bay, and refused to budge.

"The weekend's over," Oscar said. "Our suitcase is packed and in the car. We've got to go."

Although Rosa did not respond, Oscar was sure she understood the message and he tried again.

"I'm due back in the office tomorrow morning, and if I'm not at my desk I'll lose a day's pay."

When Rosa ignored his appeal and gazed obstinately out the window at the bay, Oscar sought the help of the people at the Indian Camp, who spoke to her to no avail. He then enlisted the help of Clem, who went inside and spent an hour with her.

"She's making her home here at the Indian Camp and she doesn't care whether you stay or go," he said when he came out of the shack.

"But what about my job? My career? I'm a diplomat. I'm Canada's first Native diplomat. I have a responsibility to fight for oppressed people everywhere. I can't let them down! I can't spend the rest of my life at the Indian Camp when the world needs me!"

"That's for you to decide," Clem said. "But if you choose your career over Rosa, your mother and I will look after her for you."

"I don't want to argue with you, Clem," Oscar said, "and I can't stay here waiting for Rosa to change her mind. Maybe spending some time here would be good for her. After all, she's come back to life since she arrived. I'll send you the money, and I'd appreciate it if you could keep her supplied with rice, beans, cooking oil, and bananas, as well as the occasional fresh fish and look in on her from time to time to be sure she'll be all right."

"I'll do that," Clem said. "And I'll ask your mother to give me a hand in delivering a few cords of dry split hardwood to the shack in the early fall so your wife can cook her meals and keep warm when the weather turns cold."

PART 4

1958 TO 1962

Chapter 9

AUSTRALIA AND ITS ABORIGINAL PEOPLES

1

The marriage is over, Oscar thought as he drove back to Ottawa through the heavy summer traffic. *She doesn't want to live with me anymore. She'd rather live in a shack at the Indian Camp instead of in an apartment in Ottawa with an indoor toilet and hot and cold running water, or in a foreign capital in a comfortable staff quarter with a servant to do the cleaning and duty-free booze and electronics. The marriage was a mistake in the first place. I was on the rebound from Claire and drinking heavily when I met her and didn't know what I was doing.*

The next day, Oscar called on his staffing officer and said he wanted to leave on posting as soon as possible. "I've been stuck in a dead-end job for two years and it's time I was out in the field again. I'll go anywhere."

"But what about Rosa? You can't go on a posting with a sick wife."

"She's fully recovered, and she's decided to remain in Canada close to my mother who's going to keep her company."

"Well, okay, Oscar, if you're sure about that. We've got an opening for a first secretary in Canberra. I'll send a telegram to the high commissioner to see if he'll take you. It'll be a hard sell given your record in Colombia."

❖

Oscar found that his reputation had preceded him when he reported for work at Canada's high commission in Canberra, Australia's capital two hundred miles into the interior, southeast of Sydney. Robert Evans, the high commissioner, was a shy, tall, good-humoured individual with an enormous and wholly bald head. If asked, people who knew him well would probably say that he was an honest man who treated everyone, whatever their station in life, the same way. If pressed to provide more information, they would likely add that his personal priorities were his faith, his family, and the monarchy — in that order.

After his service in the Great War, the man who would become Oscar's superior had enrolled in Knox College to train to become a Presbyterian minister, but had developed an interest in international affairs and switched to Honours History and joined the Department on graduation. In the course of his long career, he had emerged as one of Canada's most distinguished foreign policy practitioners, working for more than a decade at Canada's mission to the League of Nations in Geneva and for another decade as deputy undersecretary in Ottawa. He had then gone on to a succession of world capitals as a head of post. In all his years of service, he never lost his frugal Calvinist instincts. For example, he always felt vaguely uneasy at having a car and driver at his disposal and insisted on opening his own door and sitting in the front seat. When he and his wife were alone, they ate with the household staff in the family dining room. Only the most inexpensive of wines were served at official functions, and guests often left dinner parties at his house hungry. And certainly no one would have dared tell an off-colour joke in his presence.

The high commissioner was aware of the scandal Oscar had caused in Colombia, and when the Department requested his permission to send him to his mission, his first instinct was to say no. Fortunately for Oscar, Evans had come to know Reverend Huxley when they were both students at Knox College, and when he saw in Oscar's personnel file that he had lived in Port Carling, he decided to write his old friend to seek his views.

"Oscar had a difficult childhood, lost his grandfather in a fire, and was turned away by his mother when he was only thirteen," Reverend Huxley told him in his return letter. "My wife and I took him in and ensured he received a good high-school education and he paid us back many times over with his friendship. I am aware that he developed a drinking problem during his posting to Colombia, and for reasons of his own that I do not question, he has separated from his wife. I nevertheless believe he can still do great things with his life. I hope you give him a chance to prove himself."

❖

"Go right on in, the boss is expecting you," Ruth Oxley, the secretary to the high commissioner, told Oscar when he went to introduce himself on reporting for duty in early September.

"Sit down here at my desk. We need to talk," said Evans when Oscar poked his head around the door. "I won't bite you."

As Oscar sat down, Evans got up and walked over to the picture window that looked out over the high commission gardens.

"So you're the terrible Oscar Wolf who caused so much trouble for Georges Leroux over there in Colombia," he said, gazing out the window. "Georges and I go back a long way even though he's a generation behind me in the Department. He's a good man, but he never learned how to manage his staff. Lets them walk all over him. That's one reason he never made it to the top ranks and has spent his career in Latin America where the only thing that interests the government is trade promotion. Tolerated behaviour I wouldn't have put up with for a minute."

Without turning around to face Oscar, High Commissioner Evans reached into his pocket and extracted a neatly folded white handkerchief, removed his glasses, and set to work vigorously polishing the lenses.

"Beautiful day, isn't it, Oscar," he said, continuing to look out the window. "Just think, we never get winter here. At least not winter as we know it in Ottawa. I love the Australian spring. Cool and fresh in the mornings and hot and dry in the afternoons. Beautiful rose gardens. Never a cloud in the sky. We would die for a day like this in Canada.

"Now, Oscar," he said, turning and blinking at him through his newly cleaned glasses, "I won't stand for the shenanigans you got up to in Bogota."

Without waiting for an answer, Evans stuffed his handkerchief back into his pocket and picked up from a side table a silver-framed photograph of Queen Elizabeth II shaking hands with him. In it, he was wearing a dark grey morning coat with tails, light grey tie, dark grey vest, and striped pants, and he was bowing, smiling and accepting the graciously proffered hand of Her Majesty.

"I love all the members of the royal family, past and present, Oscar," he said. "But I have the greatest love and respect for Queen Elizabeth. I admired her work as a driver during the war and her courage when her father passed away and she had to replace him as monarch. Around that time, I was working directly for the minister and he let me go with him to attend her coronation at Westminster Abbey. And later, here in Australia, I was fortunate to meet her in person when she was on a royal tour and have my picture taken with her when she received the Commonwealth high commissioners in audience at Government House.

"I don't suppose you've ever met Her Majesty, Oscar," he said, setting the photograph down gently on the table.

"No, I haven't," Oscar replied. "But I once met her father, King George VI."

"You would have never forgotten the occasion if you had," Evans said, paying no attention to what Oscar had just said. "The royal family have a soft spot in their hearts for Indians, you know."

"It was at Buckingham Palace at the end of the war," Oscar said, continuing his story. "There were a dozen of us, from Canada, the United Kingdom, Australia, and New Zealand. We had all been awarded the military cross and there was a ceremony at Buckingham Palace where the king pinned the medals on our tunics and shook our hands. He didn't say anything, but his eyes were sad."

"Yes, indeed, the kings and queens of England, especially Queen Victoria, have had special ties with our Indians for hundreds of years," Evans said, continuing his monologue. "The treaties were signed in their names and today they never miss a chance to attend a pow wow and wear eagle feather war bonnets when they make official visits to Canada. But I suppose you know all that.

"Now let's get down to business," he said, pulling up a seat beside Oscar, touching his knee and continuing to speak without pause. "You have a drinking problem, but it's not your fault, you were born that way. Canadian Indians are like Australian Aborigines, incapable of tolerating alcohol. And that's why you must promise me that you won't touch a drop of any alcoholic beverage as long as you work for me at this mission."

"I'll do my very best, high commissioner. I'll do my best," Oscar said.

"And there's something else, Oscar," Evans said, after looking at him doubtfully and getting up and walking over to look once again out the window. "You don't have a monopoly on moral outrage. A lot of us in the Department feel just as strongly about the racism in the world as you do. But we are diplomats sent abroad to promote Canadian interests and not missionaries trying to save the souls or change the ways of foreign societies. There will thus be no solo expeditions to remote settlements to find fault with Australia's policies toward the Aborigines. I also learned a long time ago that in our profession, it's always best to work with people to get them to change their ways and not just hector them to do better."

2

Some months later, the high commissioner summoned Oscar to his office. The vice chancellor of the University of New South Wales had called to say he had learned there was a Canadian Aboriginal diplomat on staff at the Canadian High Commission.

"Apparently there's a lot of interest in Australian universities on the condition of indigenous peoples around the world, and he wants you to go down to Sydney and speak to an academic conference about the Canadian experience. Can I trust you to stick to the facts and not embarrass the high commission or the Canadian government if I let you go?"

"You can count on me to support government policy," Oscar replied.

"I hoped you'd say that," the high commissioner said. "And if you continue to think that way, maybe you'll get your career back on track."

❖

The following week, the university conference room was filled to overflowing when Oscar took the floor. Although the topic of his speech, "The History of Indian–European Relations in North America Prior to and after the Age of Discovery," was unexciting, many professors and students had come to see a genuine North American Indian in the flesh. Oscar stuck to the facts, describing at great length the Beringer ice-age land bridge from Asia, Indian culture in the pre-contact period, the extinction of the woolly mammoth, projectile points, burial mounds, late archaic pottery, spears, bows and arrows, corn, potatoes, squash, the Hopewell tradition, and Iroquoian torture techniques. He went on to review the cultural and economic impact on the First Peoples of explorers, missionaries, traders, and settlers, listed all the Indian-White wars from the sixteenth to the nineteenth centuries, the role of Indian tribes in the War of 1812–1814, and brought his lecture to a close just as the Dominion of Canada was coming into being in 1867.

Most people left before he finished speaking, and the first question by an attendee reflected the dissatisfaction of those who remained.

"That's all well and good, Mr. Wolf, but we know all that. Can't you tell us something a little more personal? How have you suffered from this history of colonization?"

"Frankly, I haven't suffered personally," Oscar said. "I went to a good school, served honourably in the army, went to university after the war, and joined the Department of External Affairs and served abroad at the Canadian Delegation to the United Nations in New York and at the Canadian embassy in Colombia before being posted to Australia."

"But surely there's more to it than that," someone said. "Don't your people live in slum-like reserves just like our Aborigines?

Aren't they denied the vote just like the black people here? And what about those residential schools?"

"If you want," Oscar said, "I can describe to you how my own people have adapted to the modern world," and he painted for them a rosy picture of the way of life of the people from the Rama Indian Reserve and the Indian Camp, emphasizing the first-rate relations they maintained with the surrounding white people and their communities. But as he was telling them about Jacob and his father and all the other Indian men who had had fought and died in Canada's armies in two world wars, someone yelled, "For God's sake, mate, are you just a yes man or do you have a mind of your own?"

Oscar countered by rambling on about manidos, water monsters, witches, bannock, sucker moons, strawberry moons, Windigos, bearwalkers, starvation in the pre-contact period, Nanibush, the Milky Way, souls, shadows, Madji Manitou, the Creator, the muskrat, the grain of sand, Tecumseh, Louis Riel, the *Amick*, the Dump Road, and someone named Clem. The few surviving members of the audience got up and left before he finished his account of the anthropological significance of the white dog feast.

The next morning, eating breakfast in his downtown hotel room, Oscar read in the *Sydney Morning Chronicle* a detailed account of his presentation that concluded with an editorial comment:

> *Mr. Wolf's lecture at the University of New South*
> *Wales last night was somewhat confusing. The gist*
> *of his talk seemed to be that Canadian aboriginals*
> *and the white people of Canada had found ways*
> *to establish and maintain harmonious racial rela-*
> *tions. If that is what he meant to say, and if what*
> *he meant to say is really true, perhaps Australia*

could learn something from the Canadian model
to apply in dealing with our aborigines.

High Commissioner Evans will be pleased, Oscar thought, and he decided to celebrate. For the rest of the day, he took in the sights, visiting Harbour Bridge and Bondi Beach and dropping into art galleries to look at examples of Aboriginal art. He went into several museums and joined groups of schoolchildren examining wonderfully mounted skeletons of Aborigine people in glass cages alongside the bones of other animal species that had become extinct after the arrival of the first settlers in 1788, such as the King Island Emu, the Roper River Scrub Robin, the Grey-headed Blackbird, the Sharp-snouted Day Frog, the Desert Rat-kangaroo, the Crescent Nail-tail Wallaby, and the Tasmanian Tiger.

Oscar was enjoying himself so much that the time passed quickly and he found himself in the late evening in the neighbourhood of Kings Cross, a part of the city where red lights lit up the entrances to all the bars. Oscar knew very well that members of the Canadian Foreign Service should not enter such establishments, but he was thirsty and went into one anyway, fully intending to spend only as much time as it took to down a glass of ice-cold Coca-Cola and depart. He sat alone at his corner table, breathing in the smell of cigarette smoke, testosterone, draft beer, sweat, cheap perfume, and air freshener, while thinking back with nostalgia to the bar in San Diego before the war where he used to throw drunks out onto the streets for a living. Then, out of the gloom came a tall, wide-hipped, dark-skinned woman about twenty years old wearing high heels, a blouse so low-necked that her ample breasts were almost entirely exposed, and a skirt so high up on her legs it would have been obscene had she not been a prostitute dressed for work.

I hope she's not going to sit down here, Oscar thought. *I'm still a married man and I'm getting my life together.*

But the woman wiggled her rump and sat down, studiously avoiding eye contact with Oscar in case he should tell her to leave. Still looking away, she smiled silently to herself, reached into her rhinestone-studded handbag, and pulled out a package of cigarettes. Holding it up close to her eyes, she examined it with such great attention one might have thought she had never seen anything like it before. Her scrutiny over, she tapped the package with the index finger of her left hand until a cigarette popped out. She then extracted it delicately with her right hand, lit it, slowly drew in the smoke, and, as she exhaled, took Oscar's hand in hers and looked into his eyes.

"Hello, John," she said.

Oscar did not answer because his eyes were fixed on a waiter carrying a bottle marked Dom Perignon approaching his table. He was well aware he should tell him to go away and bring him a glass of Coca-Cola. He also knew he should tell the prostitute to stop bothering him and leave. But at that moment, he thought only of the champagne and how much he wanted to taste it. He watched mesmerized as the waiter screwed off the cap, set the bottle and two glasses down on the table, and walked away. Oscar filled a glass, raised it into the air and gazed at it, still fighting his desire to take a drink. He had become a heavy drinker to forget Claire and to prevent a return to the depression that had plagued his life in California and in the early years of his wartime service. But it had not come back when he had given up alcohol as a condition of his posting to Australia, and now that he thought about it, neither had his brooding about Claire. He was cured, he was sure, and could drink again. He took a sip. It was a cheap sparkling wine but he didn't care, for after the first swallow, he needed another drink right away.

"Aren't you going to offer me a drink?" It was the prostitute demanding he pay some attention to her. He would give her a drink and then tell her to go away, Oscar thought. It was the polite thing to do.

But one glass led to another and soon the bottle was empty and the prostitute was still there. "Order another one and we can get to know each other as we drink it," she said.

Oscar looked at her more carefully and came to the conclusion his guest looked an awful lot like Rosa when he first met her on the bank of the Meta River in Colombia, when she still looked like the Indian princess of his dreams. He ordered another bottle and decided he wanted to get to know his guest a little better.

"My name is Ann Kumquat, John," she told him as they drank, "but you can call me Anna. All my customers call me Anna."

His inhibitions and common sense gone, Oscar told her his name and said he was a first secretary at the Canadian High Commission in Canberra. "I gave a lecture at the University of New South Wales last night," he added. "It got a glowing review in the *Morning Chronicle* and I think my high commissioner will be pleased."

"Why that's fascinating, John," she said, squeezing the biceps of his right arm with one hand and waving at the waiter to bring another bottle of plonk with the other.

"I hope you don't mind, but I call all my customers John," she said as the waiter opened the bottle. "It's easier to keep track of you that way."

After they finished the bottle, Anna took him upstairs, where she ordered yet another. Then, as Oscar repeated to her with great enthusiasm the entire lecture he had given at the university, she nodded attentively and gobbled down two buckets of oysters, a two-pound steak smeared with Vegemite, three orders of fish and chips with tartar-sauce, and two slices of toast. When he woke up the next morning, the money in his wallet and Anna were gone.

After visiting the local branch of his bank and withdrawing a thousand dollars from his account, Oscar returned to the establishment, where the manager, after glancing at the money in his wallet, charged him a thousand dollars for five bottles of fake Dom Perignon, four buckets of oysters, a three- pound steak smeared with Vegemite, and five orders of fish and chips with tartar sauce. But he didn't count the toast.

"When do you think I could see Anna again?" Oscar asked.

"She usually comes to work around ten o'clock," the manager said. "She's popular with the clients, and so if you want to spend time with her, you better get here early."

Oscar went to the bank and withdrew another thousand dollars, everything he had left in his account. And when he was in bed with Anna that night, he asked what had led her to become a prostitute and to steal money from her customers.

"The answer should be obvious," Anna said. "I want your money."

❖

When Oscar went back to work, the high commissioner came by his office. "I just received an interesting call from the secretary to the Cabinet. He told me that the government was planning to announce the establishment of a Royal Commission on the Status of Aborigine Peoples to tackle the issues facing the indigenous peoples of Australia once and for all. It's supposed to travel around the country to examine conditions on settlements, conduct consultations, and prepare a final report with recommendations. He also said he had read the story in the *Morning Chronicle* on your lecture with great interest, and had drawn it to the prime minister's attention. They agreed that you could make a valuable contribution to the commission's work by providing the commissioners with insights, based on Canadian practice, on how to uplift the Aborigines in this country. He wanted to know if you would be prepared to take a leave of absence and join their staff."

Oscar was delighted. Royal commissions, he knew, paid their employees high salaries and benefits, a lot more than he was making as a first secretary. If he could obtain the job, he would be able to see Anna as often as he liked.

"Personally," Oscar said eagerly, "as a Canadian and Aboriginal person, I've been deeply troubled ever since I arrived in this country by the way Aborigine people are treated. That's why I made it a priority in my work to read as much as I could on Aborigine issues in case I was ever asked to be a member of an Australian Royal Commission on the Status of Aborigine Peoples. I even developed close relations with a young Aborigine woman in Sydney named Anna. I wanted to hear her story to better understand her people."

"That's all very good, Oscar. You are certainly industrious. But I'm a little worried Ottawa might not let you go. It's not often governments allow their officials to participate on commissions of other countries."

But Evans need not have worried. The Department was flattered the Australians would want one of its officers to work for them, and when Oscar left to join the commission a week later, the high commissioner shook his hand and said he would go far.

The three members of the Royal Commission — Chairman Reverend Gregory Mortimer of the United Methodist Church, Father Adrian Murphy of the Roman Catholic Church, and Captain Mary Fletcher of the Salvation Army — held their first meeting in early June. As their first order of business, they asked Oscar to provide them a briefing on the situation of Aboriginal people in Canada. They had all read the press report on his talk in the Sydney *Morning Chronicle* and wanted to hear more.

"I would be happy to do so," Oscar said, "but I think you would learn a lot more if you were to visit Canada, talk to ministers and officials, visit an Indian reserve, and generally see for yourselves the model we have developed to deal with indigenous peoples."

The commissioners and their Australian advisers thought Oscar's idea was a good one. Delegations of Australians and Canadians had been making fact-finding missions to each other's country for years to share their experiences in governing their large, sparsely populated nations. It just made good sense to learn from the Canadians the secrets to their success in accommodating the Aboriginal peoples living in their midst.

High Commissioner Evans welcomed the initiative and contacted the Department of Indian Affairs to make the arrangements. When he told them the idea for the mission had come from Oscar, and sent them a copy of the press report on Oscar's talk at the University of New South Wales, they were delighted. They could not have written a better explanation of the state of aboriginal affairs in Canada, they said, in a message back to the high commissioner. And having noted in Oscar's presentation on the state of bliss prevailing at the Indian Camp at Port Carling, they planned to take the Australians there as part of their visit to Canada.

But before the delegation left for Ottawa, the first stop in its program, Evans asked Oscar to come to see him.

"This initiative of yours has the potential to strengthen Canada's ties with Australia, but it could go wrong if the visitors were to come away believing you had misled them. And so," he said, after pausing a moment, "I want you to remember what I told you when you were posted here. As a civil servant who has sworn an oath of allegiance to Her Majesty the Queen, you are obligated to defend and promote the interests of Canada and to portray it in the best possible light at all times. Whatever you do, never say anything that might undermine the expert opinion of ministers and their officials during their briefings."

3

The day after the delegation arrived in Ottawa, the minister of Indian Affairs hosted a lunch in their honour. Afterward, Deputy Minister Larry Happlebee chaired a series of briefings modelled on the talk Oscar had given at the University of New South Wales. They were, however, in such depth that it took them the rest of the afternoon to finish. The commissioners did their best to stay awake while members of their staff, including Oscar, took careful notes to be entered into the record. Happlebee then opened the floor to questions.

"Thank you, Deputy Minister," Reverend Mortimer said. "I'd like to start off by saying that the Aborigine people of Australia are complaining that they have no inherent right to their traditional lands. They say that it is unfair of the Australian government and courts to claim Australia belonged to no one when the settlers arrived. Some people are saying we should have followed your example and negotiated treaties with our Aborigine tribes. What do you think?"

"You would be making a terrible mistake," Happlebee said. "We negotiated treaties with tribes across Canada throughout the nineteenth and early twentieth centuries and it worked out well for us because the Indians were illiterate and believed anything told to them. And we never had any intention of honouring them anyway. It was just an easy way to take their lands without having to fight wars with them like the United States and South American countries like Argentina and Chile. But today, they're launching lawsuits and we'll have to give the country back to them if we're not careful."

"There was a time in the history of our country," Reverend Mortimer said, "when many well-intentioned people thought Aborigines, especially the young women, should be sterilized. The thought was that in so doing, Aborigines would be weeded out of the gene pool and the Australian race improved. There isn't much support for such practices in Australia today, but we would be interested in your views."

"The government of Canada has traditionally not been involved in human breeding programs," said Happlebee. "We leave that to the provinces; it's a federal/provincial jurisdiction issue. But if I may provide my personal views, I think Hitler gave the science of eugenics a bad name. And that's a pity because some very interesting efforts are quietly going on in Alberta at the moment where government doctors are improving the racial stock by tying the fallopian tubes of female mental defectives, poor people, and Indians when they find themselves in hospital for other reasons."

"What has been the reaction of the women?"

"Why there's been no reaction, no reaction at all. And that's because we don't tell them what the doctors are doing."

"Australian governments," Father Murphy said, "have been removing the babies of Aborigine mothers and white fathers for generations and raising them in institutions where they are trained to be useful servants for white people. Some people think the practice is cruel since the children never see their mothers again and they call them the 'stolen children.' Others firmly believe everyone benefits: the children are educated and assimilated painlessly into Australian society and Australians obtain a ready supply of cheap labour. The commission would appreciate your frank views on our policy. Do you think its disadvantages outweigh its advantages?"

"The benefits, of course, outweigh any possible drawbacks," said Happlebee. "But you don't go far enough. Our preferred option is to take the children of Indian couples from their homes, by force if necessary, and send them away to special Indian residential schools. And when they come home, usually after ten years, they function as well-educated leaders of their communities."

"How so?" said Fletcher. "Perhaps you could explain."

"We start from the premise that Indians are endowed with souls but are not as human as white people. If they were, they would have invented the wheel, composed sublime symphonies, and built great cities before the arrival of the fur traders and settlers."

"Many people in Australia share that assumption," Reverend Mortimer said.

"I don't like to boast, but we Canadians are proud of the fact that for almost a century we have been running one of the world's most innovative programs to turn these people into real humans. The concept is simple. We use education to re-program their brains and wipe out the savage parts of their psyches."

"You mean you brainwash them?"

"Brainwashing has such a negative ring to it, don't you think? We prefer to call our approach re-education."

"I imagine that with such an expenditure of money and effort, there must be many Indians going on to university."

"Oscar, of course, is one of our graduates, and I am sure there are others. They just don't come to mind at the moment."

"But let's hear what a genuine Indian has to say. Tell our guests how a residential school gave you your start in life," he said, turning to Oscar.

"Yes, Mr. Happlebee," Oscar said, standing up and earnestly and untruthfully addressing the Australians. "Were it not for attending residential school, I would have spent my life hunting and fishing and living like a barbarian. My residential school training re-educated me and made me the man I am today. It prepared me to join the army, fight in some of the bloodiest battles of the war, attend the University of Toronto, and go on to a career in the Department just like any white Canadian. As a matter of fact, my grandmother and my mother went to residential schools, as well, and their lives were changed forever."

❖

The next morning, the commission boarded a chartered bus and travelled over the Algonquin and Muskoka Highlands to the Indian Camp, carefully converted into a Potemkin village for the day. Organized in advance by the Indian agent from the Rama Indian Reserve and the mayor of Port Carling, the visit accomplished all the government's objectives. Eighty Native men, women, and children, three hundred white villagers, and six hundred tourists and day trippers off the steamers were waiting when the bus travelled over a road quickly bulldozed over the ridge and down to the Indian Camp. As the commissioners came down the steps, eight drummers and singers, in the dress of nineteenth-century Apache warriors but really Mohawks from a reserve in the south of the province, began to pound a pow wow drum and to sing and wail laments of welcome. Reverend Huxley stepped forward and offered an ecumenical prayer of welcome, and as everyone in the crowd nodded their heads in agreement, emphasized that God and the Creator were one and the same, and that Indians and white Canadians, and maybe Aborigines and white Australians, could learn much from each other on spiritual matters.

The chief of the Rama Indian Reserve had been told that if he did not cooperate, the funding for his reserve would be cut. So, outfitted in the ribbon shirt that he usually wore to pow wows, he made an impassioned speech in Chippewa telling the commissioners that the Indian agent on instructions from his department in Ottawa had come to the Indian Camp ahead of time to tell the people that it would be good for business to pretend they had no grievances against the government. Then, raising his arms, he strode to his car, his head uplifted in a scowl, and drove away. Oscar immediately broke into applause, and the commissioners, who didn't understand a word of what the chief had said, and were too polite to ask for a translation, followed his lead.

The next person to speak was the mayor of Port Carling, and he earnestly praised the historic ties that had unified the people of the Indian Camp and Port Carling dating back to the arrival of the first settlers to the region.

"Our grandfathers and grandmothers came to the wilderness of the District of Muskoka many decades ago find a community of savages squatting on Crown land. And although they were pagans and living in a state of ignorance, they helped those first settlers to become established and formed friendships that persisted long after they voluntarily vacated their lands. And the strength of that relationship," he said, looking directly at Oscar, "was confirmed one night in late June 1930 when a heartless arsonist, like a thief in the night, set fire to the business section of the village. The two founding peoples of Canada and Port Carling, Indian and white, fought together in a show of interracial partnership to save the buildings, but with only buckets of water to combat the merciless flames, the battle was lost. Two brave souls, one Indian and one white, died in the fire. And one day, perhaps not too far in the future, the constable will come knocking on the door of guilty party and bring him to justice."

Uncomfortable with the direction of the speech, Oscar looked away from the mayor, who was now shaking his finger at him and saying that the arsonist should do the right thing and surrender to the law. Rosa, Oscar saw, was standing at the back of the crowd with a group of Native women including his mother, but he wasn't yet ready to meet and tell her their marriage was over. After the mayor finished speaking, the women moved forward, on a signal from the Indian agent, to drape braided wreaths of sweetgrass, like Hawaiian leis, around the necks of the delighted visitors.

"Come with us," they said. "Come and see how the Indians live in Canada."

Leading the commissioners to their shacks, they explained that these were just their summer cottages, and sold them quill boxes and toy tomahawks, all heavily marked up in price for the occasion.

"It's a shame we can't show you our homes back on the reserve," they said. "We all have electricity, hot and cold running water, double-pane insulated windows, mail order furniture, framed copies of Group of Seven paintings, indoor plumbing, and television sets, just like the other Indians in Canada."

They led them to the shore where their waiting children rushed on cue into the water and began splashing each other, shouting out with cries of joy.

"Access to sand beaches for all Indian children is an inherent right written down in the treaties between our grandfathers and the Crown and enshrined in the Indian Act," the women said. "Just like access to clean water, sanitation, medical services, and equal education with mainstream society, which we are all privileged to enjoy."

❖

Later that evening, after accompanying the highly impressed Australians to their accommodations at a nearby luxury lodge on the shore of Lake Muskoka where a special performance of Indian dancing and drumming was on the program, Oscar returned to the Indian Camp to ask Rosa for a divorce.

Rosa, however, had different plans, and did not invite him inside when he knocked on the door of the shack.

"I've been expecting you," she said, speaking in fluent Chippewa. "Nothing much seems to have changed: I can smell the alcohol on your breath from where I'm standing. You're probably as big a drunk as you ever were," she said, stepping outside. "And it was mean of you to abandon me and never to write."

"But you don't know how to read."

"Your mother would have read the letter to me, if you had made the effort."

"But you don't speak English."

"No, I don't, but I now speak Chippewa and your mother would have translated it for me. You are just making excuses for your bad behaviour. Your mother told me how bad a son you were, always lost in a world of your own, spending all your time at Old Mary's listening to nonsense instead of helping out around your own house, leaving her all alone each spring and running off with your grandfather to the Indian Camp, and hanging around with white kids from the Port Carling school and being too good to associate with your own people. She told me things so terrible I can hardly believe them, like setting fires and betraying the white people who took you in after you went begging at their door. You don't even own this old shack but your wonderful mother let me live here and she comes over all the time to teach me Chippewa and to show me how to cook bannock and to give me lessons on making moccasins and quill boxes."

As Rosa's tirade continued, Oscar tried to stop listening and asked himself what could have happened to turn the sad, submissive, innocent girl from the jungles of Colombia into a nagging Chippewa wife? Perhaps it was punishment from the God he did not believe in for all those awful choices he had made in life? More likely it was the result of his mother saying nasty things about him behind his back.

"Your mother said we should get a divorce," Rosa was saying, advancing toward him and forcing him to retreat. "She said I'd never be happy with you. She said you could never be trusted. She said she'd take care of me but you'd have to send half your salary to support me."

Did Rosa just say divorce? Did this woman he first saw swimming naked in the Meta River, did this ungrateful individual he had saved from the death squads, did this refugee he had brought from the blood-soaked land Colombia to peaceful Canada just mention divorce? He should have been happy, for that was exactly what he wanted, but his feelings were hurt. He should have been the one to tell her their marriage was over. It wasn't fair.

"But you're Catholic, Rosa, you can't get a divorce."

"I'm not Catholic. It was you who made me get baptized so we could go through that form of marriage in Bogota. I don't know what you thought you were doing when you took me away from my own country. You never understood that I am a real person with real feelings. Now go away and don't come back. My lawyer will be in touch with yours."

While still smarting from his encounter with the new Rosa, Oscar walked away from the shack happy that his marriage would soon be over and he was free to devote himself to Anna. But just to be sure he was doing the right thing, he went to see Clem, although it was now the middle of the night.

"It's hard for me to say anything," Clem said, his voice frail after Oscar woke him up and explained his problem. "Rosa's been helping your mother take care of me and I kinda look upon her as a daughter. She looks a bit like Stella when she was younger, don't you think?"

4

Oscar returned to Australia determined to marry Anna as soon as his divorce with Rosa was finalized.

"I love you, Anna," he said when he was drinking with her once again in the room above the bar in Kings Cross. "I want to meet your mother and all your relatives, I want to know the story of your people, and I want to remove you from your sinful life and bring you home to the Indian Camp."

"Who do you think you are, a social worker?" Anna said. "I'm a working woman and not at all ashamed of the services I provide."

"But we're both Aboriginal persons; that should count for something."

"To me, you're not an Aboriginal person. You're just a client, but I'll sell you all the love you will ever need as long as you have the money. And if you want, I'll tell you the history of my people, but I charge for my services by the hour."

Oscar said he'd like to hear the story of her people, and Anna began by saying that millions of years ago, when the dinosaurs roamed the earth, a kind lady named Lucy lived with her family somewhere in Africa. They were all very happy there, but then one day it got very cold and glaciers crept across the land from south to north forcing Lucy and her family to leave their village and flee northward to safety. Eventually they reached the Jordan Valley in the Middle East where they had to make a decision. Should they turn west and go to Europe? Should they turn east and go to Asia? Or should they make boats and go to Australia? To Lucy's great disappointment, they were unable to agree among themselves and the family split up, with some becoming Englishmen, some Red Indians, and the rest Aborigines. Lucy went to Australia with the ones heading south in boats across the ocean, and that is why the Aborigines say she is the mother of their homeland.

Then the years went by, Anna said, and Lucy died and was mourned by all the people. More time went by, millions of years went by, and the Aborigine people lived in harmony with nature and with each other, never quarrelling, treating their women like goddesses, and eating only fruit that fell from the trees. They built a great city at Ayers Rock, in the middle of the desert, with running water, indoor toilets, and fast food restaurants and colour televisions. Then invaders arrived from England on sailing ships and by trickery defeated the troops of the last emperor and told everyone that Aborigines weren't human beings. But the white invaders hadn't managed to destroy all traces of Aborigine culture. To this day, the invisible Aborigine city of Angora, inhabited by people who worshipped a religion called the Dreaming and constructed by the same engineers who built Machu Picchu in the Andes Mountains, lies hidden inside Ayers Rock. The Australian government knows it's there and sends out military missions led by the Australian Special Forces to find and destroy it, but always without success.

Every night for a week, Anna told Oscar the same strange version of history, always saying, as she ended her story, that she wanted to visit Angora someday. And every night, as Oscar listened to Anna talk her nonsense, he sank deeper and deeper into an alcohol-fueled gloom, feeling guilty about his unfair treatment of Rosa and, most of all, about his collaboration with the high commissioner and Indian Affairs in hoodwinking the Australian commissioners. Finally he could take no more and he went downstairs to the bar where he drank and drank until the sun rose in the east over the Tasman Sea. He then got up out of his chair and made his way to the door, desperate to make it back to Canberra to tell the commissioners that there was an Aborigine city hidden in Ayers Rock.

❖

Oscar woke up in the ward for the clinically insane at the Canberra General Hospital. When he opened his eyes, he saw white padded walls, a white ceiling, white bars on the windows, and white sheets on a white bed. He didn't know where he was or who he was. The door opened and a white-haired man with a white beard, wearing a white laboratory coat came in and sat down in a white chair. Oscar believed he was in heaven and in the presence of God.

"I see you're awake," God said. "How are we doing today?"

Oscar remembered who he was and thought God was about to ask him to account for all the shameful things he had done in his life, for which he had no adequate explanation. Afraid he was about to be sent directly down to the fire and brimstone of Hell, he threw himself on the mercy of the Almighty, saying, "I'm sorry,

I'm sorry. Don't send me down there. I'm really a good person even if I don't believe in you. I went to Sunday school as a boy and that should count for something."

But as he spluttered on, he vaguely remembered drinking cheap Australian sparkling wine and running out into the street with a message of some sort to deliver to the commissioners.

"The police found you sitting on the sidewalk outside a bar in Kings Cross," God said, ignoring Oscar's incoherent stammering and speaking to him as if he were a child. "You were yelling something about finally understanding the meaning of the Dreaming. You've been here under heavy sedation for a month. I hope you have health insurance."

At that moment, Oscar understood that he wasn't in the presence of the God he wasn't sure existed.

❖

On being discharged from the hospital, Oscar found the following letter on his desk when he went back to work.

Dear Oscar,

I am writing to tell you some terrible news. Clem McCrum died in his sleep. In accordance with his long-standing wish, he was cremated and there was no funeral service. Your mother and Rosa paddled down the Indian River, said a prayer, and threw his ashes into Lake Muskoka at the foot of the Manido of the Lake. Although he was not a believer, I think Clem would have approved. Please let me know if there is anything I can do to help.

Your friend,
Lloyd Huxley

Although Clem's passing came as no surprise, given his deteriorating state of health, the news still came as a great blow. Oscar rushed down to Kings Cross to seek consolation in the arms of Anna, but Anna, his dear Anna, having met a dozen or more new clients, each one of whom she called John, no longer had time to see him. He took to hanging out in Aboriginal bars and drinking beer with his new friends, all of whom confirmed Anna's version of Aboriginal history, but only if he paid for the drinks.

Reverend Mortimer, worried that Oscar was no longer coming to work and unable to reach him by telephone at his apartment, asked the police to track him down. In short order, an officer of the Australian Federal Police paid a call on Anna. Afterward, the secretary to the Australian Cabinet spoke to High Commissioner Evans, who summoned Oscar to his office and asked him to take a seat.

"I have the sad responsibility to advise you," he said, smiling uncomfortably and glancing at the photograph of the queen for reassurance, "that Reverend Mortimer has asked me to tell you that your employment with the royal commission has been terminated for reasons I have no desire to enter into. And since we have filled the position you occupied here at the high commission with another officer from Ottawa, you should leave at the earliest opportunity for headquarters. Someone there will know what to do with you."

5

When Oscar reported for duty in Ottawa in September, he expected to be fired. Instead, his staffing officer greeted him with a friendly handshake and compassionate smile and asked him to take a seat on the sofa he used only to receive important visitors.

"We are proud of you, Oscar," he said, handing him cup of coffee and sitting down beside him.

Oscar usually felt patronized when white people said they were proud of him. It was as if he was a child being told by adults that he had exceeded their expectations. But this time, he took it as an indication that High Commissioner Evans had not told headquarters about all the disgraceful things he had been up to over the summer.

"I think the Australian commissioners found their trip to Canada useful," Oscar said, guessing the Department had received a positive report on the visit.

"The Department of Indian Affairs can't say enough good things about your initiative to bring the Australians to Canada, about your interventions during the briefings and your excellent proposal to have them visit the Indian Camp at Port Carling. I have to confess I had never heard of that little reserve or Port Carling before. Both places are now on the radar here in Ottawa."

"I was just doing my job," Oscar said, shifting uneasily in his seat.

"You're just being modest, Oscar. I have a message on my desk from the high commissioner saying that in all his years of service abroad, he had never met an officer who had made as big an impression in such a short time as you did on the locals. Apparently the secretary to the Cabinet even called him about you. He said the visit you organized to Canada will have a long-term effect on Australian policy toward the Aborigines. It seems the Aussies are considering setting up residential schools to be run by members of the mainstream clergy on the Canadian model. And everyone Down Under credits you for giving them the idea."

"But that wasn't my intention," Oscar said. "That wasn't what I wanted at all. I really don't know what to say," he stammered. "I wouldn't have proposed the fact-finding mission in the first place if I had thought the commissioners would have considered such a thing."

"There you go again, selling yourself short. You deserve all the credit. The high commissioner mentioned one small thing in his message, however, that I feel I must bring to your attention, particularly in view of your record in Colombia. Apparently you occasionally drank too much and acted in a somewhat curious manner. Evans added that since you are an Indian, and as is well known, Indians are physiologically incapable of tolerating spirits, your strange behaviour should be overlooked. He said it would be worth asking you, however, to give up drinking as long as you are in the Department."

"I know I'm an alcoholic," Oscar said. "But I haven't had a drink since I left Australia, and I'll be on the wagon from now on."

Chapter 10

SOUTH AFRICA AND APARTHEID

1

This time the funeral would be different from the others Oscar had attended since arriving in South Africa. This time it would be held at the Soweto football stadium and not at Regina Mundi Catholic Church or St. Paul's Anglican Church. This time the security police had killed twelve young anti-apartheid activists, shooting them in the back as they fled the scene of a banned demonstration, and those churches were too small to accommodate the number of mourners expected to attend. Each funeral he had gone to as Canada's official representative had left him heart-sick and he wanted a break from the emotionally draining duty.

"Why don't you send someone else?" he asked Canada's ambassador to South Africa, Stuart Henderson. "I've covered more than my fair share of these things since I arrived."

But Henderson, who liked to adopt an avuncular tone when dealing with his staff, did not agree. "Look here, Oscar," he said.

"We've had this conversation before. The Department in its wisdom sent you here because it thought that you could do a better job in representing Canada at the funerals of black militants than one of its white diplomats. And now you're trying to wiggle out of your job when Ottawa has such high expectations for you. So do what you were posted here to do, or get on a plane and go home!"

Ambassador Stuart Henderson was not a career diplomat like most Canadian ambassadors and high commissioners who join the Department as junior officers and work their way through the ranks to the top. He had been a major fundraiser for the party in power in Ottawa just after the war, and as his reward the prime minister posted him to head up, successively, Canada's consulates in Detroit, Los Angeles, and Chicago. At the end of the fifties, the prime minister sent him as head of post to South Africa as a sort of farewell gift before retirement. When he sent his political ally to South Africa, however, Canada's leader did not know that Henderson usually accepted as true what the friends he made at the local golf clubs, service clubs, and churches told him, whatever the facts of the matter.

And if he hadn't had political connections at home, he wouldn't have lasted long in his new post. Soon after his arrival in Pretoria, he sent a lengthy cable back to the Department that shocked everyone who read it. "The Afrikaners are reasonable people doing reasonable things," he said in his message. "I know this for a fact because some very nice senior ministers of the government and a pleasant and well-informed gentleman who is head of an organization here with the amusing acronym of BOSS have taken the time to brief me on apartheid over drinks at the country club and at intimate dinners in their homes. I am convinced that the reason so many people outside South Africa condemn apartheid is because they don't understand the benefits of separate development for South Africa's blacks, whites, Asians, and coloureds."

Aghast, the Department recalled him to headquarters and tried to explain to him the iniquities of racism in all its forms. "Don't rely on government ministers for your information. Get to know the people fighting for their freedom. Stay away from BOSS; it's the South African Bureau of State Security responsible for torturing and killing political prisoners. And come up with an initiative or two to show Canada's solidarity with South Africa's oppressed communities."

To Henderson's credit, although he continued to play golf and share meals with his Afrikaner friends, including the gentleman from BOSS, he made an effort to cultivate the people leading the fight against apartheid, although they suspected he was only going through the motions when he professed support for their cause. He even came up with the idea of asking the Department to send, as a sign of solidarity, an officer to the mission to attend the funerals of militants killed by the South African security service. He was disappointed, however, when Ottawa sent Oscar to do the job, since he didn't like Canadian Indians any more than he did South African blacks, Asians, and coloureds.

The Department and its senior officers expected their juniors to obey their orders without question, and so Oscar assured Ambassador Henderson that he would attend the funeral. But he was deeply unhappy. And not just because of the emotional cost. Some months before, Canada's prime minister had made two impressive decisions to advance the cause of human rights in Canada and the world. He announced that Canadian Indians would be allowed to vote in federal elections, and he became a leader in the fight to have South Africa expelled from the Commonwealth because of its apartheid policies. But then he ruined everything by getting up in the House of Commons and saying that "there would always be a light in the window" welcoming South Africa back to the civilized world when the time was right. All it had to do was to behave toward its downtrodden peoples with the same just and humane policies followed by Canada in its treatment of its Indian population.

The prime minister's remarks made Oscar wince. Surely Canada's leader must have known that the South Africans had modelled their apartheid policy, at least the part providing for the herding of black people into townships and homelands, on Canada's system of Indian reserves? Surely he must have been aware of the pitiful state of the people on the reserves?

Making him feel worse, despite his best efforts, was the fact that he had made no friends in the anti-apartheid movement. When he made his calls on Anglican bishop Jonathan Tumbula and other black leaders, they had greeted him warily, almost as if they thought he had come to give them lessons on how to deal with oppressive white governments. He did not know that they, in fact, believed his posting was a stunt, devised by Ambassador Henderson to cover up his insincere support for their aspirations.

2

Oscar backed his car out of his garage in a whites-only leafy suburb of Pretoria early on the morning of the funeral and drove through streets lined with purple jacaranda trees and red and pink hibiscus bushes to the motorway to Johannesburg. Before he left Ottawa, perhaps because he had seen so many pictures in *National Geographic* of smiling khaki-clad bronzed game wardens in national parks and people frolicking in the Indian Ocean surf, he had assumed South Africa would be hot and sunny twelve months of the year. But he had been mistaken. The summers on the veldt were hot and dry interspersed with violent thunderstorms, and the winters, more often than not, were cold and damp. The day he set out for the funeral was one of the bad ones. A steady drizzle was falling, the clouds were low and dark, and the air smelled heavily of coal smoke drifting in from cooking fires in the nearby black townships.

The traffic through Johannesburg was not as bad as he expected, but slowed to a crawl when he started down the road into Soweto. Crowds of people, singing "Nkosi Sikelel' iAfrika," the anthem of the banned African National Congress, clogged the way. Oscar had been haunted by the beauty of the song's melody ever since he heard it at the first funeral he attended. It reminded him of the hymns sung in Chippewa back on the reserve when he was a boy, and he learned the words in English to be able to sing along at funerals.

> *Lord Bless Africa*
> *May her horn rise high up*
> *Hear Thou our prayers and bless us*
> *Descend, O Holy Spirit,*
> *Descend, O Holy Spirit.*

A mile from the stadium, a line of heavily armed police was stopping and turning back traffic. Oscar eased his vehicle off the road, parked on a patch of bare land, and continued on foot. Passing through a police line was usually an ordeal. A sullen police sergeant would study the document issued to him by the Ministry of Foreign Affairs identifying him as one of the several first secretaries on staff at the Canadian embassy, entitled on strict basis of reciprocity to all the rights and privileges as outlined in the Vienna Convention on diplomatic relations between states, including but not specifically spelling out his right to live in a leafy whites-only suburb of Pretoria despite his dark-brown skin and black hair and eyes. The policeman would motion Oscar to follow and lead him to a mobile police headquarters and leave him standing outside for an hour, presumably in an attempt to humiliate him, before returning his document and telling him he was free to go.

This time, Oscar seemed to have been expected. An officer stepped forward before he reached the barrier and, brushing aside Oscar's identity card, said "That won't be necessary today, sir. Just follow me." And he escorted him through the lines and saluted him when he said goodbye with what might have been a sarcastic smile. *Maybe the police have decided to go easy on the mourners today,* Oscar thought. *Maybe no one's going to get hurt afterwards on the way to the cemetery.*

Oscar joined the jostling crowd pushing to gain entrance to the stadium, and once inside, made his way to a group of people gathered around a raised platform in the centre of the field.

"Ah, Mr. Wolf," said Bishop Tumbula, who was to lead the service, "I was afraid you weren't coming. Unfortunately, it appears that you may have to represent the diplomatic corps today. None of your colleagues has as yet put in an appearance. Perhaps they are afraid things may get out of hand."

Oscar shook the bishop's hand and quickly made the rounds, introducing himself to the dozen or more priests and ministers who were to participate in the ceremony, expressing his sympathies to the families of the deceased and saying a few words to people he had met in less public occasions and who belonged to banned organizations. Everyone, except the members of the families of the victims, who did their best to smile, looked through him when they accepted his hand.

3

One week later in his hospital room in Pretoria, Oscar emerged from oblivion with a great headache, his jaw wired shut, his right arm in a cast, and Ambassador Henderson looking at him from a seat beside his bed.

"How are you, Oscar?" the ambassador asked, speaking quickly and coldly, making it clear he just wanted to get an unpleasant task over with as soon as possible. "I guess you can't talk, so I'll fill you in. The police brought you here two days ago. They said they found you after the funeral outside some bootlegger shebeen place in Soweto where loose women hang out and where they sell beer. They say you got drunk and fought with the patrons over a woman. They've even provided signed affidavits from the proprietor to back up their case. You can just imagine the damage this affair has done to the embassy. Everybody in the country is talking about it. The newspapers, including the South African liberal press, are saying Canada made a colossal mistake in sending a drunk to its embassy in South Africa at such a delicate time. Some enterprising journalist even dug up the press coverage in Colombia and Australia on your escapades during your postings to those countries.

"I'm on your side, of course, as is headquarters, at least publicly, but only because we have to be, only because the good name of Canada is at stake. Back home, the CBC, which always takes the side of the underdog whether justified or not, gave the story lead coverage in its national radio and television news, claiming you had been hard done by. Editorial writers across the country, who have never had anything positive to say about developments in this country, have accused the South Africans of using the same sort of brutality against a Canadian Indian as they use against their black people. The prime minister has defended you in the House of Commons, saying you were set upon by thugs from the South African security service who then concocted a story claiming you had been beaten up in a house of ill-repute. I hope for your sake it turns out he's right. Now I must go. Someone from the office will drop by to see you every day until you are fit to travel. Then you are going home. The Department has cancelled your posting."

Oscar saw the ambassador's lips moving but the ringing in his ears was so loud he couldn't hear what he was saying. It was evident that he was agitated and angry about something. He was probably upset that one of his first secretaries had been injured. Oscar wasn't surprised. He had always suspected that under his pompous exterior, Henderson had a big heart.

In the coming days, the staff of the Canadian embassy took turns visiting Oscar, and as the noise in his ears diminished, he learned to his distress that he was the major figure in a diplomatic row between Canada and South Africa. Still not able to remember what had happened, and unable to talk, he could only listen as his colleagues, some in all seriousness, others unable to suppress their laughter, and everyone believing that he was in some way responsible for his own misfortune, did their best to cheer him up.

Disconnected images then began to flash through his mind. He once saw twelve coffins draped in the flag of the African National Congress being borne onto the football field on the shoulders of seventy-two pallbearers. Another time, he was in his car frantically turning the key in the ignition and trying to escape someone or something that was trying to seize him and do him harm. The engine would not start and he got out and raised the hood only to find that the distributor coil was missing and to face the same policeman who had escorted him through the police lines.

"We've been waiting for you," the policeman said, before the scene faded away. And yet another time, he saw coffins being dumped onto the ground with bloody corpses spilling out and people running, and he heard screaming and he smelled tear gas and coal smoke and felt cold rain on his face.

Each day fresh visions appeared: Bishop Tumbula angrily haranguing the crowd before turning and pointing an accusing finger at him as if he were in some way personally responsible for the deaths of the militants; a policeman, armed with a heavy leather whip, beating an old woman until he, Oscar Wolf, intervened, pushing the policeman to the ground and kicking him repeatedly in a blind rage until driven off by other policemen who lashed him with their whips until he outran them and escaped; drinking homemade corn beer in a garishly lit front room of a shebeen and joking and laughing and frolicking around the floor to loud African music with a six-foot-tall, wide-hipped black woman with enormous breasts who had come out of nowhere to sit on his lap.

One week later, the pieces of the puzzle were in place and Oscar remembered what had happened. Pallbearers carried coffins draped with the flags of the African National Congress onto the football grounds as massed choirs of women sang "Nkosi Sikelel' iAfrika." There were hymns, prayers, and speeches, and the crowd roared. The drizzle became a downpour and the smell of coal smoke became overpowering. Pallbearers hoisted back onto their shoulders the coffins and raised their right arms in clenched salutes before exiting the grounds followed by the clerics, the members of the banned organizations, the people in their thousands, and Oscar Wolf. Policemen forced their way into the crowd to attack the pallbearers and force them to drop the coffins and spill the bodies onto the ground. Fighting broke out and Oscar went to the rescue of an old woman only to be chased back to his car where South African policemen were waiting for him. They punched and kicked him and he fought back, at first holding his own before being overpowered by superior numbers. He broke loose and ran through the streets until he found refuge in a shebeen, where, despite his decision never to touch liquor again, he had a drink, or two or three or four, with someone who reminded him of Anna while he waited for an opportune moment to flee Soweto. He fought with someone who said something bad about his mother and was thrown outside into the rain. The rest he did not remember; he did not want to remember.

4

Two weeks after the police dropped him off at the hospital in Pretoria, Oscar's doctors removed the wires from his damaged jaw and told him to go home.

"I'm giving you a week to pull yourself together," Ambassador Henderson said when he went by to see him later in the day. "Then you got to pack up and leave for Ottawa where your family can take care of you."

But Oscar didn't want to go back to Ottawa. He saw himself eating greasy grilled cheese sandwiches for lunch in some grungy restaurant in downtown Ottawa, sharing an office with someone who had just returned from Paris or London and who spent his time talking about all the important people he had met, going home in a crowded bus after work to a one-bedroom, sparsely furnished apartment, cooking dinners of wieners and beans and piling the dirty dishes one on top of the other in the sink, and spending his evenings alone watching NHL hockey matches and television game shows. And dashing from his bus stop through sleet and snow over slush-covered sidewalks to his overheated domicile in winter or lying in bed with the windows open in summer as Ottawa sweltered through yet another heat wave.

If only he had challenging work to look forward to on his return, none of this would matter. But he would be sent once again, he was sure, to another dead-end job for the indefinite future. No, for all its problems, South Africa was where Oscar wanted to spend the next three years of his life.

"But I don't have family in Ottawa," Oscar told the ambassador. "I'd rather stay here and finish my posting where I can continue to help fight apartheid."

"That's quite out of the question," the ambassador said. "You know how they are at headquarters. Once a decision has been taken, there's no going back on it. I think they've found someone to replace you."

"It would look like I was a coward, running away after a beating. That wouldn't be good for Canada's image," Oscar said. "I wouldn't be able to attend any more funerals if I stayed, but there are lots of other things around here I could do. Maybe I could work in the consular section, helping Canadian tourists who land in jail or have lost their passports. Maybe I could find something to do in the administration or trade sections."

Ambassador Henderson did not welcome these suggestions.

"When headquarters proposed that you come here to take on this delicate job, I warned it that something like this could happen if it posted someone with your background here, and I was right. You let alcohol get the better of you when you were in Colombia and it is no secret you drank too much in Australia. The Department seemed to think you had stopped drinking when it sent you here, but it was wrong and you've made a fool of yourself and your country again here in South Africa. I can't trust you and you must leave."

"I admit I'm an alcoholic," said Oscar. "But with the exception of the incident in Soweto, I've been on the wagon since I left Canberra. Surely an alcoholic is allowed to make a mistake from time to time. I've learned my lesson."

"I don't believe you, Oscar. Once an alcoholic, always an alcoholic, they say. And there's more to it than that. You never got along with the people you were supposed to be helping. Although I'm sure you would never admit it, that's because you think you're better than everyone else around here when you're really not.

That's why your contacts, including your diplomatic colleagues, laugh at you behind your back."

"But with respect, sir, those people sent me flowers and get well messages after the police assaulted me," said Oscar.

"Are you sure it was the police who assaulted you, Oscar?" the ambassador said. "I think there's some truth to the allegations that you drank too much after the funeral and got into some sort of brawl. At least that's what I'm hearing from my friends in BOSS."

"If you really think that's what happened," said Oscar, "why haven't you told headquarters?"

"I haven't done so," said the ambassador, "because I'm aware of some of the things you've been up to in the past and I don't want to ruin your career any more than it has been already. So why don't you just leave and make a fresh start elsewhere, out of my sight. I'll give you a good report for your file if that will make you happy."

Chapter 11

REDEMPTION

1

Oscar was disappointed but not surprised when his direct appeal to the undersecretary to be allowed to stay in South Africa remained unanswered, and he returned to Canada to his old job in Information Division. His colleagues, however, who had not forgotten his behaviour during his previous postings, were outraged that he would defile a funeral by getting drunk afterward and tarnishing the name of the Department and would hardly speak to him. And it was not just the officers, clerks, and secretaries in Information Division who treated him this way. No one, not even the cleaners, parking-lot attendants, security guards, or commissionaires, people he used to look upon as friends, people who would drink coffee and gossip with him in the cafeteria, wanted to be seen with him. He was not invited to provide his views on the status of indigenous people around the world when United Nations Division organized a colloquium on the subject in the auditorium. No one asked him to spend weekends hiking and canoeing with them at their cottages in the Gatineau Hills. And perhaps it was just his imagination, but the waiters in the modest restaurants he frequented apparently knew who he was and took pleasure in seating him at tables located next to the toilets.

The only person in Ottawa, it seemed, who was unaware of Oscar's missteps and ostracism within the Department was Joseph McCaully, the minister of External Affairs. He came from an old moneyed family in Toronto that for generations had faithfully allocated ten percent of its income to good causes abroad and in Canada. Before the war, as patriarch of the family, McCaully had directed the bulk of the donations to supporting missionary work in China. After the expulsion of the missionaries by the communists in 1949, he began contributing to the fight against malaria and bilharziasis in Africa. At home, he helped fund soup kitchens, housing for the homeless, clubs for lonely men and women, as well as shelters for abandoned dogs and cats. Keenly interested in the latest intellectual developments affecting church doctrine, he attended workshops in the basement of his progressive church on the different approaches to existentialism by Sartre and Camus, on the nuances in the positions of Karl Barth and Rudolph Bultmann to Biblical criticism, and on the theological significance of the big bang theory.

Although he was an active member of a charitable organization that donated used clothing and books to Indian children in the north, McCaully scoffed at the idea Canada's Indians were as badly off as the people in Africa. The only Indians he had met were the people at the Indian Camp at Port Carling. They always smiled when they sold him the beaded moccasins and quill boxes decorated with sweetgrass that he liked to hand out to friends and family at Christmas. They laughed at the harmless little jokes he told as he made his purchases, and he assumed they liked him and were happy, and if they were happy, he supposed that all Indians liked white people and that all Indians were happy. Not that he gave the matter much thought.

An incident occurred in the summer of 1935, however, involving an Indian teenager, which had bothered him for years. Like many of his Forest Hill friends, he had a summer home on Millionaires' Row on Lake Muskoka where he was a neighbour of the Fitzgibbons. He was drinking a Bloody Mary on their front veranda at one of their popular Sunday brunches when their daughter, Claire, led a young man up the stone steps to introduce him to her parents. He had never forgiven himself for laughing when the hostess refused to shake the outstretched hand. He had never recovered from the shame of snickering when the unwelcome guest, his hand shaking from nervousness, spilled some freshly squeezed orange juice onto the floor. And to his everlasting dishonour, he had not protested afterward when the Fitzgibbons made ugly racist remarks about Indians and announced their intention to put a stop to the friendship between their daughter and the boy.

In the years that followed, McCaully had tried to keep track of the young man whose name he found out was Oscar Wolf. The local Presbyterian minister said he had left for California in the fall of 1935 to become a famous actor playing Indian roles in movies, had later joined the army and won medals for bravery, and still later had joined the Department. The last he had heard of him was one summer day several years earlier when he had come into Port Carling in his motorboat from his place on Millionaires' Row to do some shopping to find the village filled with visitors. He made enquiries at the general store and learned that Oscar had brought a delegation of Australians to the Indian Camp for some reason or another. And if he hadn't had to get back to receive some guests, he would have found a way to speak to him privately and ask him to forgive him for his unacceptable behaviour at the Fitzgibbons' brunch.

After he was appointed minister of External Affairs following a by-election victory in the spring of 1961, McCaully asked about Oscar.

"He joined the Department in 1948, served abroad in New York, Bogota, and Canberra, and is now a first secretary at our embassy in South Africa," the undersecretary told him.

"I remember him well," the minister said. "He was just a delivery boy at the general store at Port Carling in the mid-thirties when I met him. He apparently had a lot of hardship in his life, losing his father in the Great War and his grandfather in a fire. I'm so pleased that he's done so well, joining the Department and becoming one of its star officers."

"You're absolutely right, minister. You're absolutely right as always. And I used to think that way about him as well."

Then one day in the fall of the same year, the prime minister took McCaully aside after Question Period in the House of Commons to tell him that leaders at international summits no longer sought him out to shake his hand. "I think it's because the world is forgetting the role I played in the fight to expel South Africa from the Commonwealth. People have short memories and we have to keep coming up with fresh initiatives if I'm to continue my fight to keep up Canada's international standing."

When the minister told him that current Canadian efforts in South Africa were largely confined to sending a first secretary to funerals in Soweto to show solidarity with the opponents of apartheid, the prime minister shook his head in frustration.

"Attending funerals is all very well and good, McCaully, but we need to do something more dramatic, something that will bring credit to Canada, something I can talk about at international summit meetings, something that will make the other leaders want to shake my hand."

The minister spoke to the undersecretary, who spoke to his deputy, who was someone so brilliant that when confronted with

an exceptionally difficult foreign policy problem, he could immediately think of a half-dozen mutually exclusive solutions to it.
He in turn convened a working group of like-minded brilliant
officers to meet with the minister to find an answer to his request.
In the ensuing discussions, someone proposed cutting off the
imports of South African diamonds, but someone else said newly
engaged couples in Canada and around the world would protest.
Someone proposed banning the import of titanium used in the
manufacture of aircraft fuselages, but someone else said Canada's
aerospace industry would collapse. Someone proposed asking
NATO to cancel its secret military alliance with South Africa,
but someone else said Western security would be jeopardized if
NATO warships couldn't use the Walvis Bay and Simon's Town
naval bases in the event of a war. At that point, the meeting ended
and the participants, pleased at showing off their knowledge of
South African matters to the minister, left the room.

Not knowing what to do, unaware that most policy discussions in External Affairs ended inconclusively, and anxious to
come up with something to satisfy the prime minister, McCaully
thought of Oscar.

"Bring that young man back from Pretoria," he told the
undersecretary when he next saw him. "He'll have the answer."

"It just so happens his posting to South Africa is over," said the
undersecretary. "He's back at his old job in Information Division."

❖

"The minister wants to see you right away," a secretary told Oscar,
poking her head around the door of his basement cubbyhole
office. Since no minister had ever displayed the slightest interest in
seeing him in all the years he had spent in the Department, Oscar
thought he was about to receive bad news. Maybe the minister
wanted to reprimand him in person for his errors of judgement in
South Africa. Maybe he would tell him to clear out his desk and

find another job elsewhere. On the elevator, the other passengers paid close attention when they saw him push the button for the third floor where the minister and his staff had their offices. Other than the undersecretary, it was highly unusual for career civil servants to visit that floor. "I guess they're finally going to get rid of you," a particularly unfriendly colleague told him.

When the door opened, Oscar saw before him the austere reception area where for generations ministers of External Affairs had received visiting foreign dignitaries and ambassadors making their courtesy calls. To his right was a dim corridor lined with dusty black-and-white photographs of former ministers and colour prints of members of the royal family on tour in Canada. And standing directly in front of Oscar and smiling broadly was Minister McCaully himself.

The minister reached in and pulled Oscar toward him, embraced him and pumped his hand forcefully, saying "Oscar, Oscar," with such passion, Oscar was afraid he was going to kiss him. "Come with me," he said as he led him into his office. "This is where I work," he said, pointing at a battered pedestal desk and a swivel chair. Behind the desk was a table piled high with old newspapers and tattered files with red "secret" stickers on them. On the wall behind the table, the eyes of the Fathers of Confederation wearing top hats and swallow-tail coats followed visitors to the room unsmilingly from a faded black-and-white picture. To the right, a long-condemned and unused grey marble fireplace dating from the previous century held a bouquet of dried flowers as decoration in its grate.

"Please take a seat," the minister said, leading him to a hard-backed sofa along the left wall in front of a narrow opaque lead glass window overlooking a lawn and the Centre Block of Parliament. As a butler poured coffee, the minister said, "I don't suppose you remember me."

Oscar did not remember him and instinctively didn't like him. Why, he asked himself, was the minister being so nice to him when everyone else in the Department was convinced he was a menace to the conduct of Canada's foreign relations? He listened distractedly as the minister added that he had a summer home on Lake Muskoka and did his shopping at the general store in Port Carling. "I know the Indian Camp well," he said, getting Oscar's attention. "I even used to know your grandfather before he died in that terrible fire back in 1930. I used to buy moccasins from your mother. You spent your summers there, didn't you? That's what the local people have told me."

Oscar nodded, not liking the fact the minister knew so much about his family and early life. It formed part of his background that he had kept hidden from the Department. "Yes indeed," the minister said, "I have been visiting the Indian Camp to buy souvenirs and fresh fish for as long as I can remember. But I haven't asked you here for old time's sake. I wanted to discuss with you something terrible that happened in August 1935 that has bothered me since that time."

Oscar put down his coffee cup and looked at the minister who was wiping away tears from his eyes. Was the minister referring to his role in helping Clem blast a crater in the dump road? He thought that incident had been forgotten years ago.

"You must wonder why I've waited twenty-six years for this moment," the minister said. "I was at the summer home of the Fitzgibbons when Claire brought you to brunch. I was one of the guests who laughed when you spilled orange juice on the floor. I said nothing to defend you when Hilda and Dwight Fitzgibbon later said nasty things about your people. For twenty-six years I have lived with this guilt on my conscience. For twenty-six years, I have wanted to tell you I was sorry and to beg your forgiveness."

"I've altogether forgotten about that incident," Oscar said, lying politely. "You did nothing wrong anyway. That's the way people behaved in those days — today, as well, for that matter. But if it makes you feel any better, I'm happy to forgive you."

"Thank you, Oscar. You don't know how important that is to me. I'll be able to sleep with that sin off my conscience. Now I'd like to get your help on something else. Before I get started, however, I wanted to tell you how pleased I am that you did something with your life. How many other poor Indian boys abandoned by their mothers after losing their caregiver grandfathers in a fire would have accomplished what you have? Imagine, going on to graduate top of your class at high school, becoming an actor in Hollywood, winning medals for bravery in the war, and becoming one of Canada's most distinguished diplomats and a leading expert on the United Nations, Colombia, Australia, and South Africa. I am so proud of you!"

Oscar looked away from the minister. Someone else was saying he was proud of him! Someone else was patronizing him! Someone else was giving him credit for something he had or hadn't done. The only things he had done well in his life were drinking, womanizing, and fighting. He was now really upset and about to tell him to shut up, even if that meant he would be fired on the spot.

But before he could get the words out, the minister said, "I understand, Oscar, that you've just come back from South Africa, and I need your help on a delicate matter. I just asked the undersecretary to prepare a proposal to put Canada in the lead among the nations of the world in the fight against apartheid — something that would enhance the status of the prime minister when he attends summit meetings. But he was unable to come up with anything, despite his best efforts and those of his experts. Do you think you can help me?"

Oscar was in no mood to help. "I hope you don't misunderstand me," he said, after looking at the minister dubiously for a few seconds, "but are you mainly interested in getting some good publicity for the prime minister or are you truly interested in helping South Africa's black people?"

"What a strange thing to say, Oscar. Of course I'm interested in helping the people," the minister said. "I want you … I want you," he said, searching for exactly the right way to express his instructions, "I want you to come up with an initiative to ensure the oppressed black people of South Africa know that they are not alone in their misery."

"Then I have an idea you might wish to consider," Oscar said, "It's something I've thought about a lot ever since I came back from Pretoria. The prime minister is on record as saying that South Africa should adopt with its black people the same just and humane policies that Canada follows in its treatment of its Indian population. If you agree, Minister, I'll organize a visit to a typical Canadian Indian Reserve for a group of influential South African journalists. They'll see for themselves the results of Canada's just and humane policies toward its Indian people. I guarantee their reports will cause a sensation."

"If I remember right, you brought a group of Australians to the Port Carling Indian Camp for the same purpose a few years ago, didn't you?"

"That's right, Minister, but this time I'll take them to a more representative reserve."

"Then you just go ahead and do it, Oscar, go right ahead. I want to make the prime minister happy."

2

At Pickle Lake airport in northwest Ontario in early January of the following year, Sergeant Penny of the Ontario Provincial Police approached the passengers who had just come off a chartered flight. "Are you the people from South Africa I'm supposed to escort to the Osnaburgh Indian Reserve?" he asked. Oscar detached himself from the others and said that was indeed the case. They were journalists who were going to take pictures and write stories for their newspapers back home, and he was their liaison officer.

"I hope you know what you're doing," Penny said. "Today's welfare day on the reserve and everyone's spent the morning in Pickle Lake stocking up on booze. They're now on the way home on the road and you're not going to like what you see."

❖

"What did I tell you," Sergeant Penny said during the ten-mile bus ride to the reserve, as the journalists took pictures of men and women sitting half buried in the snowbanks as they drank from open wine bottles and tried to flag down passing cars for rides. Others were staggering along the snow-covered highway carrying cases of beer. Still others were sprawled out drunk on the side of the road.

"It's against the law for anyone to drink alcohol in public places, but I don't have enough men to put a stop to it. And if we ever tried to take their booze from them, we'd soon have a drunken mob on our hands. So we just let them go to it and hope they don't hurt themselves or each other."

The journalists by this time were puzzled: Was this the typical Indian reserve Oscar had promised to show them? Was this the reserve where they would see a model of progressive community development and harmonious race relations?

"Are you sure we're going to the right place?" someone asked Oscar, as they drove past a woman, no more than eighteen years old, up to her knees in the snow and being sick in the bushes.

"Of course I'm sure. My mother's family comes from here and I've been here before," he replied, thinking it preferable not to mention that his previous visit was a quarter of a century ago.

The bus turned off the highway and passed a cemetery overflowing with coffin-size mounds of snow and dirt on the side of the road leading to the band office.

"What happened here?" someone asked when the bus driver stopped to let them out to take pictures, "a disaster of some sort? A big fire or bus crash?"

"No," said the sergeant, "more than three hundred people have died violent deaths on this reserve in the past ten years, and those are just some of the graves. They lost their traditional way of life and never learned to live in the modern world. They barely get by hemmed in on the reserve, and have nothing to do, day-in and-day-out, year-in and year-out. None of the mines and logging companies that took their lands wants them as workers, and the government gives them tiny welfare payments, just enough to keep them living in squalor. They take their frustrations out on themselves, beating and murdering each other when they're drinking. They lie down on the railway tracks, hoping to get run over. They sleep in the snow hoping they will never wake up, and sometimes they get their wish. The teenagers don't even wait until they're drunk before they kill themselves. These reserves are hell-holes.

"The suffering of the children bothers me the most," he said. "They're sent away each fall at the age of six to residential schools, and are only allowed home for visits at Christmas and during the summer. If the parents won't let them go, we have to seize them and deliver them to the schools. It's a part of the job no cop up here likes. Can you imagine what it would be like to live in a community of two thousand people where your hunting grounds have been taken from you and there are no children over the age of six and where every time a baby is born, you have to live with the knowledge that someday the government is going to come and take that child away. And how could you endure knowing that the teachers are beating and raping your sons and daughters and there's nobody around to tuck them in at night?"

The band office was a battered building with boarded windows and with graffiti messages scrawled on the outer walls saying *White Fuckers Go Home, We Want to Die*, and *Jeannie Loves Joshua*.

Runny-nosed children, scarcely larger than toddlers and wearing neither hats nor mittens, stood passively in the snow. A pack of dogs, their ribs visible, circled around the visitors as they went up the steps to the landing.

"I told the person who called that you wouldn't be welcome if you came," Chief Zebadiah Mukwah told the delegation. "We don't want outsiders coming to take pictures and gawk at our misery. So get back in your bus and leave our territory."

"But I'm not an outsider," Oscar said. "My grandmother, Louisa, came from here. And her mother, Betsy Loon, one of your Band members, is my great-grandmother. We've stayed in touch over the years and she's invited me to come and see her whenever I wanted. I'm the organizer of the delegation and wanted to show them her home."

"Well, okay, if you're Betsy's great-grandson, you might as well stay. Go on over to her place to say hello if you want, but I still don't want to talk to your delegation."

❖

Betsy was sitting in a rocking chair close to the stove standing in the middle of the room when Oscar knocked and entered her one-room shack. Two frost-encrusted single-pane windows and a lit oil lamp resting on an orange crate provided the only light. There was a bucket in one corner with human waste in it and another one on the floor near the door filled with drinking water. Half a loaf of white bread, a few cans of soup, a package of baloney, a can of condensed milk, an open container of margarine, and a jar of strawberry jam sat on the table. A dog came out from under the table growling and showing its teeth, but after sniffing Oscar wagged its tail and returned to its place.

"It's me, Granny," Oscar said, "I've come to say hello."

Betsy did not move and Oscar thought she was dead. Coming closer, however, he saw her eyes open and focus on his face.

"Caleb," she said, "Caleb, is that really you?"

"No, Granny, I'm Oscar, Louisa's grandson. I came to see you before the war."

"Oh, Oscar," she said, smiling. "It's so good of you to visit an old woman like me."

"I've wanted to visit with you for years," he said. "But I didn't have the chance until now. I've got a delegation of South Africans with me. They're from a country in far-off Africa. Could you meet them? They want to know how our people live."

"Of course, Oscar, whatever you say. I don't care where they come from as long as you know them. They're welcome to come in and take pictures if they want, but there's not much to see and not much room. But first let's have a cup of tea and talk a little. Tell me what you've really been up to since we last met."

As the others waited outside in the bus, Oscar made tea and told Betsy things about his time in San Diego, in the army, and in the Foreign Service that he wouldn't have wanted to put in his letters to her.

"Now tell me," Betsy said, after laughing at Oscar's stories, "What's the real reason you've brought these strangers to the reserve?"

When Oscar merely smiled and said nothing, she asked, "You don't know the answer to my question, do you? The Creator is still using you as his trickster to get a laugh."

"This time I know what I'm doing, Granny, and for once I know why I'm doing it."

Epilogue

The following morning, the stories filed by the journalists were front page news in South Africa. The president himself, with barely concealed satisfaction during a hastily convened press conference in Pretoria, expressed his outrage at the inhumane manner the Canadian government treated its Red Indians. "I hope," he added, "the Canadian prime minister will clean up his own act before he ventures once again to criticize South Africa's policies of separate development for its white, black, coloured, and Asian peoples."

The Canadian Press filed a report that was picked up by newspapers across Canada and around the world. Columnists from the *New York Times*, the *Daily Telegraph*, *Le Monde*, and the *International Herald Tribune*, who usually considered developments in Canada too boring to merit their notice, paid attention. In their articles, they said it would be a long time before members of the international community took Canada seriously again when it professed concern for oppressed peoples. Journalists by the dozen hurried to the Osnaburgh Indian Reserve where Chief

Zebadiah Mukwah took them on a tour, including a lengthy visit to speak to Betsy at her home, to expose the living conditions of his people. Two days later, after receiving a full report from officials of the Department of Indian Affairs, the prime minister telephoned Minister McCaully and summarily dismissed him for letting himself be hoodwinked by one of his officers. And as soon as Oscar got back to Ottawa, the undersecretary summoned him to his office and fired him.

But the opposition parties during Question Period in the House of Commons combined to attack the government, not for displaying bad judgement in facilitating the visit of a delegation of South African journalists to one of Canada's most impoverished and troubled reserves, but for allowing such terrible conditions to exist in Canada in the first place. Editorial writers demanded the reinstatement of the minister, church leaders delivered sermons, and schoolchildren waving placards condemning the government's treatment of Indian Canadians gathered on Parliament Hill. When a national campaign of prayer breakfasts began, the prime minister asked Joseph McCaully to come to see him in his office in the Centre Block and restored him to his former position.

In Johannesburg, Bishop Tumbula read the press reports and chuckled when he saw Oscar's name. Ambassador Henderson sent a personal message to his patron, the prime minister, proposing that Canada adopt a policy of apartheid along the South African model to deal with the Indians since obviously assimilation was not working; he was fired by return telegram for his pains. In the sunny breakfast nook of her Forest Hill home, Claire smiled as she read the same stories in the *Globe and Mail*. In Canberra, Reverend Mortimer, Father Murphy, and Captain Fletcher held an emergency meeting of the commission behind closed doors and quietly removed from their final report all reference to Canada and all things Canadian such as residential schools. And back at Port Carling, Reverend Huxley and James McCrum, drinking coffee together in the basement of the Presbyterian church after Sunday services, agreed that there had been a divine purpose to the Great Fire after all.

No one in the Department, however, called Oscar to cancel his dismissal, but he wasn't upset. When he had proposed taking the journalists to the reserve, he had known he would be fired when their reports were published. He wouldn't be a martyr, as he had dreamed of becoming when he was a boy, dying for his cause like Tecumseh fighting the Americans in the War of 1812, or John Brown battling to free the slaves at Harper's Ferry. But he would be offering up what was left of his career as a sacrifice to strike a blow against everyone, everywhere, who continued to deprive Aboriginal people of their dignity. That goal had been accomplished, and he would now leave Ottawa and spend his remaining years at the Rama Indian Reserve surrounded by his own people. He would wear his hair in braids. He would become friends with his mother and Rosa. He would beg the forgiveness of James McCrum for torching his store. He would apologize to Reverend Huxley and his wife for deceiving them. Perhaps in so doing he would finally atone for the harm he had done to others all his life.

Two weeks later, after cancelling the lease on his apartment and packing his few belongings into his car, Oscar left Ottawa to start his new life. It was by now late January, the sky was cloudy with sunny breaks, the snow was four feet deep in the bush, and the snowbanks were so high he couldn't see over them as he drove through the Algonquin Highlands and into the District of Muskoka. And as he drove, the words to "Shall We Gather at the River" came to him unbidden and repeated themselves over and over again in his head. But rather than being irritated by their insistence to be heard, he felt strangely happy and at peace with himself for the first time in years. It was time, he thought, to return to the embrace of the Christian God and reconnect with the Holy World of Old Mary.

Turning off the highway running through Port Carling, he took the new road that went up and over the ridge to the Indian Camp, hoping to speak to Rosa and his mother before he continued on to the reserve. To his surprise, the path to the shack had not been shovelled, and the building was encased in snow drifts that lay deep on the roof, against the door, and up to the casements of the windows. No one was living there, but he wanted to visit the old summer home of his grandfather just the same.

He parked his car, got out, and struggled through snow up to his waist to the door. Using his hands, he dug down until he found the handle, turned it, and pushed hard. It swung inward, dumping him and a load of snow onto the floor. When he tried to rise to his feet, a blinding light struck him in the face and forced him to lie back, close his eyes, and cover them with his hands. But the light radiated through his hands and eyelids and grew ever stronger, and he felt the presence of something as otherworldly and awesome in its power as the ghostly being he had encountered on first entering the shack after the Great Fire of 1930. Jacob was there in the room with him, he was certain, and not just his shadow. Somehow his grandfather had managed to come back from the Land of the Spirits to forgive his beloved grandson for setting the fire that had killed him and Lily. It was the redemption he had been seeking for more than three decades.

Opening his tear-filled eyes, he smiled when he saw that the sun had broken through the clouds and its radiance was reflecting through the windows off the snow. But when he sat up and looked outside, he saw, to his horror, the Manido of the Lake shimmering like a mirage in the light, laughing at him.

Reader's Guide

A CONVERSATION WITH JAMES BARTLEMAN

The protagonist in your first novel, As Long as the Rivers Flow, *is Martha Whiteduck, a Native woman seeking to regain her sense of self and humanity after a decade of abuse at the hands of her teachers and a priest at an Indian residential school in Northern Ontario in the latter half of the twentieth century. As we follow her touching personal story, we learn that she returned to her reserve broken in spirit, hardly able to speak her own language, and without the skills needed to raise her own children after spending so many years in an institutional setting. We learn that a suicide epidemic among Native youth has been ongoing for decades out of sight and out of mind of mainstream society among the children of residential school survivors. As we get to know Martha better, we learn about the suffering of Native people in modern Canada and their attempts to heal themselves. Do you have a similar social justice theme for* The Redemption of Oscar Wolf?

Yes, I do. Several in fact. My new novel traces the life of a Native person, Oscar Wolf, from boyhood to middle age as he seeks to find redemption for a terrible crime he committed in a fit of misguided rage against white society when he was only a teenager. Many of the underlying themes deal with Native issues, in particular the need to come to terms with the loss of ancestral lands in the nineteenth and twentieth centuries and the ongoing struggle to achieve equality in a society that looks upon Native people in stereotypical ways. But at its heart, the novel deals with issues common to everyone, whatever their racial or cultural background, such as maternal and spousal love, the desire for revenge, the search for meaning in life, anger against God and the Native Creator, Divine Providence, hubris, pride, hate, miserliness, generosity, and the need for redemption. It could be described as a parable of Native life in mid-century Canada and around the world.

Why didn't you write a book of non-fiction to deal with these tough moral issues?

A novel takes the reader inside the heads of the characters and when a character laughs, the reader laughs, when the character suffers, the reader suffers, when the character rages against the injustices of humankind and Divine Providence, the reader does likewise, and so on. And most important, the novel leads the reader to make connections and links between the fortunes of the protagonists and himself or herself and thus to broaden his or her understanding of the big issues we often think about only after midnight with our heads under the covers. Non-fiction, even creative non-fiction, cannot do that.

What led you to begin the novel with a journey and a fire?

The train and canoe journey is a metaphor for the travel in search of redemption Oscar will follow throughout his life. The fire leads Oscar and his benefactors in Port Carling to ask themselves questions about Divine Providence that are developed in the course of the novel. I began thinking about the journey and fire when I recalled two stories related to me by my mother when I was a boy of nine or ten back in the 1940s.

In the first, she told me that one magical night, when she was a girl about my age in the late 1920s, she attended the wake for a beloved member of the Rama Indian Reserve. Throughout the evening and into the night, she sang along with the others the old Christian hymns in the language of her people. She left with her father for the railway station and boarded a passenger train at midnight, arriving at Muskoka Wharf Station at the bottom of Lake Muskoka at one in the morning. Father and daughter then travelled some twenty miles by canoe to the Indian Camp located within the village limits of Port Carling where her father trapped beaver and muskrat along the Indian River and worked as a handyman at a guest house in the white village. Throughout the journey, the hymns the people sang at the wake repeated themselves time and time again in her head as she looked up at the stars on that wonderful late April night that she never forgot.

In her second story, she told me that one night in the early 1930s she was spending the summer as usual with her family and the other members of the Rama Indian Reserve at the Indian Camp, selling handicraft and fresh fish to tourists to support themselves. One predawn morning, the fire bells of the three village churches began to peal, summoning all able-bodied men to fight a fire that had broken out in the basement of the village general store. Her father and the other Native men joined the white men of the village to fight the fire, but it spread and destroyed the entire business section. Her mother said at the time that she was certain the fire was the work of an arsonist because late in the night before the fire, she had been walking along the path leading from the Indian Camp to the business section when a man ran into her in the dark and knocked her over. She thought his behaviour was suspicious since he reeked of coal oil and did not answer her request to identify himself, but instead got up and ran off.

Are all of the characters fictional?

The villagers are fictional but several of the Native ones are based in part on members of my own family. Perhaps unconsciously, I drew on the life experiences and personality of my mother in creating the young Oscar. And Stella, the mother, resembles to an uncomfortable degree my mother's mother. Pursued by inner demons after spending her childhood and early adolescence in the tuberculosis sanatorium at Gravenhurst, she took out her frustrations on her daughter. She beat her mercilessly, even hitting her with a two by four. She once drove her into the river in front of the family shack at the Indian Camp where, to my mother's revulsion and shock, a four-foot water snake wrapped itself around her body. Jacob is loosely based on my great-grandfather Fred Benson, a veteran of the Great War, who was gassed in the fighting in northern France and came home to the reserve to die, and my grandfather, Ed Simcoe, whom I remember well as a kind and compassionate person. In an act of heroism, Ed entered a burning guesthouse during the fire that destroyed the business section of Port Carling to try to rescue a tourist girl trapped in her room. He brought her out but she died of her burns.

Ed also did what he could to protect my mother from her mother, taking her with him in late April of each year when he left the reserve for the Indian Camp, just as Jacob did with Oscar. Although a child barely able to see over the top of the cookstove, my mother lit the fires and prepared meals of bannock and fried fish for her father. From the age of six to twelve, she attended the Port Carling elementary school in the months of May, June, and September. The other months of the school calendar she attended the Rama Reserve day school. She made many good white friends in Port Carling but was subject, as was Oscar, to the overt hateful racial discrimination shown to Indians from others at that time in Canada's history.

And Obagawanung? Did it actually exist?

The Native village of Obagawanung was located, as described in the novel, on the banks of the Indian River at the site of the future Port Carling in the District of Muskoka. Its chief was a shaman and veteran of the War of 1812. Vernon Wadsworth, part of a survey team from Toronto that visited Obagawanung in the early 1860s, described him and his village in two excerpts from his memoirs as follows:

> I met the Indian Medicine Man of the Ojibway Tribe, named Musquedo, at Obagawanung Village. He was then eighty years of age but strong and vigorous. He had a flag pole in front of his hut with an emblem on top to denote his vocation. He invited me to a white dog feast and other pagan ceremonies. He had a large silver medal conferred on him for bravery at the battle of Queenston Heights in 1812 in which he participated on the British side with other Indians of the Georgian Bay district.
>
> The Indian village ... consisted of some twenty log huts, beautifully situated on the Indian River and Silver Lake with a good deal of cleared land about it used as garden plots, and the Indians grew potatoes, Indian corn, and other vegetable products. They had no domestic animals but dogs and no boats but numerous birchbark canoes. The fall on the river there ... was about eight feet, and the fish and game were very plentiful. Musquedo brought us potatoes and corn and we gave him pork and tobacco in return.

When the first settlers from the Old Country arrived in the 1860s to take possession of their lands, the chief, with the help of a visiting white man, sent the following heartbreaking petition to Governor General Lord Monck to let his people stay:

> Father, we the Indians known as the Muskoka Band of the Ojibway Tribe living at our Village Obagawanung, being in the straits between Lakes Rosseau and Muskoka, desire to convey through you to our Great Mother the Queen the renewal of our dutiful and affectionate loyalty.
>
> Father, we are in trouble and we come to you to help us out. We believe that your ears are always open to listen to the complaints of your Red Children and that your hand is always ready to lead them in the right path.
>
> Father, many winters have passed since we settled here and began to cultivate our gardens. We have good houses and large gardens where we raise much corn and potatoes....We live by hunting and taking furs. We hope you will grant the wish of your Red Children, and do it soon, because the whites are coming in close to us and we are afraid that your surveyors will soon lay out our lands here into lots.

The governor general rejected their appeal, and the people were forced to abandon their homes to make new lives elsewhere.

You were a Canadian diplomat for thirty-five years, from 1966 to 2002, serving in Colombia, Australia, and South Africa as well as a half-dozen other countries. Are you Oscar the diplomat?

Not at all — although there are several similarities between us. Like Oscar, I am a direct descendant of a Native veteran of the War of 1812. John Simcoe, who was the grandfather of my great-grandmother, fought with the British against the Americans during the War of 1812, including at the battle for York in April 1813. Like Oscar, I had a white beneficiary, in my case an incredibly generous retired American businessman who funded my university studies. Like Oscar, I served as a member of Canada's Department of External Affairs. Unlike Oscar, I managed to stay out of trouble and went on to serve in a dozen overseas postings in a career lasting more than thirty-five years.

Like Oscar, I was posted to the Canadian Delegation to the United Nations, but in my case only for one session of the United Nations General Assembly in the fall of 1966 as a staff member on the committee dealing with decolonization. It was a privilege to have been present during that session at the eighteenth anniversary commemorations of the signature of the Universal Declaration of Human Rights on December 10 in the presence of its principal drafter, John Humphries, a Canadian on the International Staff. I was later posted as a junior officer to the Canadian embassy at Bogota, Colombia, as was Oscar.

There was no Claire in my life. Nor was there a Rosa, but I did take a television journalist to the hot interior of the country near the Venezuelan border to spend a few extraordinary days with an anthropologist friend who was living with a group of Cuiva Indians on the shores of the Meta River. I was able to confirm that the reports I had received about Indians being hunted down by settlers who wanted their lands were true. The journalist returned with a film crew, prepared a documentary shown in the United Kingdom, but unfortunately the Colombian government did nothing to end the killings.

During a posting in Australia, there was likewise no Anna, but I did meet with Aboriginal stolen children survivors, and had the privilege of being hosted by Aboriginal people in their community in the Northern Territory.

Like Oscar, I was assigned to the Canadian mission to South Africa, but in my case as High Commissioner in the post-apartheid era. Like Oscar, I was brutally beaten, but by a common criminal and not by the security police, in an assault that nearly cost me my life and led the government to cut short my posting. Before I left, however, I was privileged to speak to President Mandela and other members of the African National Congress about life in the apartheid era. During a lunchtime meeting with Archbishop Desmond Tutu in Toronto some years later, the Nobel Peace Prize–winner described to me a visit, organized by the Canadian government, that he had made in the apartheid era to the Osnaburgh Indian Reserve (now called Mishkeegogaming First Nation) on Lake St. Joseph on the headwaters of the Albany River in northwestern Ontario. Words could not describe his distress, he told me, when he saw the condition of the people. They were worse, he said, than anything he had witnessed in South Africa in its darkest moments. I knew exactly what he meant since I had visited Mishkeegogaming First Nation many times and knew well the people, and I thus made it the setting for the final scene of the novel.

Did you ever run into anti-Native sentiment in your years in the Foreign Service?
Not at all. Like Oscar, I worked with strong, gifted sometimes idiosyncratic colleagues who would never have thought of discriminating against anyone on the basis of race, religion, or cultural background but expected everyone to carry out their fair share of the burden of work. Moreover, I was a private person and very few of my career colleagues in the Department knew my background.

Then why did you portray Stuart Henderson, the Canadian ambassador to South Africa, as someone who supported apartheid?

Canada's ambassador to South Africa in the late 1950s and early 1960s was not a career officer. His deputy at Pretoria, Gordon Brown, who would later go on to become an ambassador himself, described him in his memoirs as someone who "was convinced of the need for the blacks to live separately from the whites." (*Blazes Along a Diplomatic Trail*, Trafford Publishing, Victoria, 2000.)

Does the Manido of the Lake actually exist and what role does it play in the novel?
The Manido of the Lake, although only appearing four times, occupies a central place in the plot. It is the incarnation in the form of a stone statue of the Creator who put Oscar on Mother Earth to do all manner of foolish things and make it laugh from time to time in a world dominated by the white man.

The Manido exists to this day at the northern end of Idlewylde Island on Lake Muskoka, where it is known locally as Indian Head Rock. Native relatives and friends who came to our old home in the 1940s in Port Carling to share a meal of fish and wild meat and to spend the evening talking with my parents used to terrify me with their stories of the bearwalker, the Windigo, witches, and the most feared monster of them all, the seven-headed serpent with eyes the size of dinner plates that had been devouring unlucky Native fishermen on Lake Muskoka since time immemorial. Only the Manido of the Lake, they would declare in hushed tones, had the power to protect the fishermen from destruction and guarantee a good catch of fish. My grandfather would never think of travelling on Lake Muskoka without making an offering of tobacco and uttering a prayer to the Manido.

Acknowledgements

I would like to first thank my wife, Marie-Jeanne, and my son Alain for reading and providing their unvarnished opinions on the manuscript.

I owe a debt of gratitude to Dr. Brian Osborne, Professor Emeritus of Geography, Queen's University, and Dr. Graham Brown, Principal of St. Paul's College, University of Waterloo, for their encouragement and helpful comments on structure.

Ed Willer, a colleague in the Foreign Service, provided his comments, for which I am grateful, on the chapter dealing with South Africa. Ed served there during the apartheid era and was responsible for representing the Canadian embassy at funerals in Soweto and elsewhere of African National Congress militants killed by the South African security services.

Lorenz Friedlaender and Ken Harley, likewise friends and colleagues from the old days in the Department, read the text and provided helpful factual suggestions. Ed, Lorenz, and Ken should not, of course, be held responsible for my portrayal of life in the Department in the post-war years.

I am most grateful to Don Antoine for his vivid descriptions of the Canadian campaign against Germany in Italy in the fall and winter of 1943. Don was a sergeant of 48th Highlanders of Canada and was mentioned in despatches and wounded in the fighting.

And finally, I thank Lieutenant-Colonel (retired) John Beswick, an officer of the Royal Canadian Dragoons during the war, for his patience in briefing me in depth on the fighting in Italy.

More Great Fiction from Dundurn

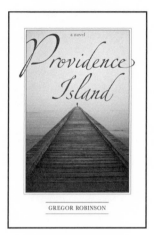

Providence Island
Gregor Robinson
978-1-554887712
21.99

Returning to bury his father, Ray Carrier is taken back to the woods and swamps that haunted his teenage dreams. He'd been enchanted by the privilege of the Miller family, especially Quentin Miller, a beautiful girl a bit older than himself. But something happened near the railway tracks that must be settled before Ray can finally achieve peace.

City Wolves
Dorris Heffron
978-0-978160074
36.95

Meg Wilkinson, Canada's first woman veterinarian, leaves her
Halifax practice after a tragedy in her private life and heads to
Yukon Territory, drawn by the sled dogs she has come to admire.
When she arrives in Dawson City in 1897, the exciting and tumul-
tuous gold rush is just getting underway.

VISIT US AT

Dundurn.com
Definingcanada.ca
@dundurnpress
Facebook.com/dundurnpress